BEASTLY RHYMES

TO READ AFTER DARK

written by
JUDY SIERRA

illustrated by
BRIAN BIGGS

Alfred A. Knopf   New York

THIS IS A BORZOI BOOK PUBLISHED BY ALFRED A. KNOPF

Text copyright © 2008 by Judy Sierra

Illustrations copyright © 2008 by Brian Biggs

All rights reserved. Published in the United States by Alfred A. Knopf,

an imprint of Random House Children's Books,

a division of Random House, Inc., New York.

KNOPF, BORZOI BOOKS, and the colophon are registered trademarks of Random House, Inc.

www.randomhouse.com/kids

Educators and librarians, for a variety of teaching tools, visit us at www.randomhouse.com/teachers

Library of Congress Cataloging-in-Publication Data

Sierra, Judy.

Beastly rhymes to read after dark / by Judy Sierra ; illustrated by Brian Biggs. — 1st ed.

p. cm.

ISBN 978-0-375-83747-0 (trade) — ISBN 978-0-375-93747-7 (lib. bdg.)

1. Animals—Juvenile poetry. 2. Children's poetry, American. I. Biggs, Brian, ill. II. Title.

PS3569.I39B43 2008   811'.54—dc22   2007006815

The illustrations in this book were created using a combination of traditional and digital methods.

MANUFACTURED IN CHINA • July 2008 • 10 9 8 7 6 5 4 3 2 1

First Edition

To lovely Maxine

—J.S.

For my own beasts, Wilson and Elliot!

—B.B.

THE LAVATORY CROCODILE

A darling baby crocodile

Departed from the River Nile,

Swam through the Gates of Hercules,

And past the great Sargasso Sea,

Into the Gulf of Mexico.

Gently paddling to and fro,

Up a river, up a creek,

Growing larger week by week,

She settled in the loathsome pool

Beneath the bathroom of your school.

When next you find you have to go,

Look first, and wave, and say, "Hello!"

Be sure to flash a friendly smile

And greet the darling crocodile,

For as I told you once before,

She's not a baby anymore.

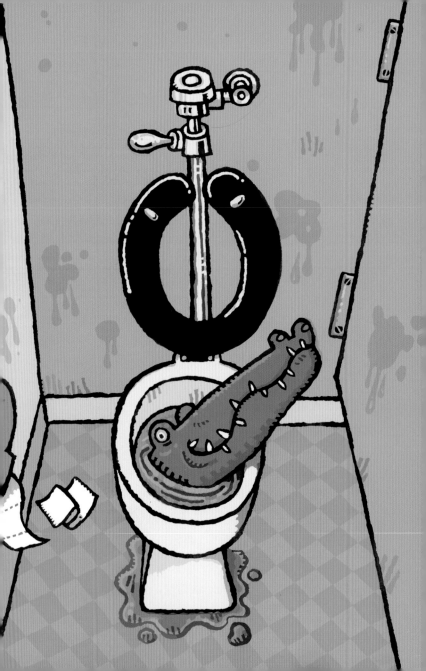

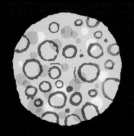

ANNIE'S BABIES

Annie's babies like to bite.

Annie's babies howl all night.

In the daytime, they're much calmer.

They are werewolves, like their mama.

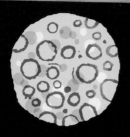

ANNIE'S BABIES

Annie's babies like to bite.

Annie's babies howl all night.

In the daytime, they're much calmer.

They are werewolves, like their mama.

PET SHOW

Oh where, oh where can my kitty cat be?

She promised to go to the pet show with me.

And all of the other nice pets will be there,

Like Beth's barracuda, and Gabe's grizzly bear,

Art's anaconda, and Kate's killer bee.

But where, oh where can my kitty cat be?

WHO IS HAUNTING THE ZOO?

Boo! Boo! Boo! **Boo!**

Who is haunting the zoo?

There's a phantom flamingo,

A windigo dingo,

An elephant skeleton, too,

A mummified moth,

The wraith of a sloth,

And a walloping were-kangaroo,

A gory gorilla,

And Franken-chinchilla,

And most of the ghost of a gnu.

It happens each fall,

As they creep and they crawl,

And the animals all

Trick-or-treat at the zoo.

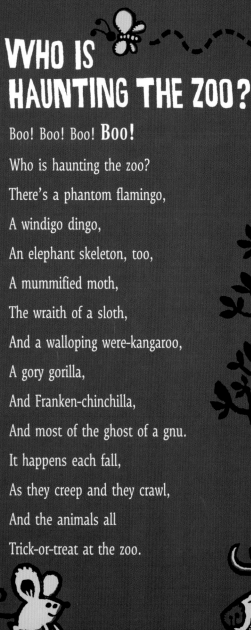

LEOPARD CHEFS

My next-door neighbor, Hilda Hitchen,

Kept two leopards in her kitchen

Who, when Hilda wasn't looking,

Taught themselves the art of cooking.

Thursday, Hilda came home late

And found a heaping, steaming plate

Of Spam with jam, and ham with mustard,

Dumplings, pies, and chocolate custard.

All appeared as if by magic,

Yet the outcome could be tragic.

When she'd eaten every scrap,

"I am *so* stuffed!" dear Hilda yapped.

"You are, indeed!" the leopards roared . . .

And slid her through the oven door.

TWISTED TONGUE RESTAURANT

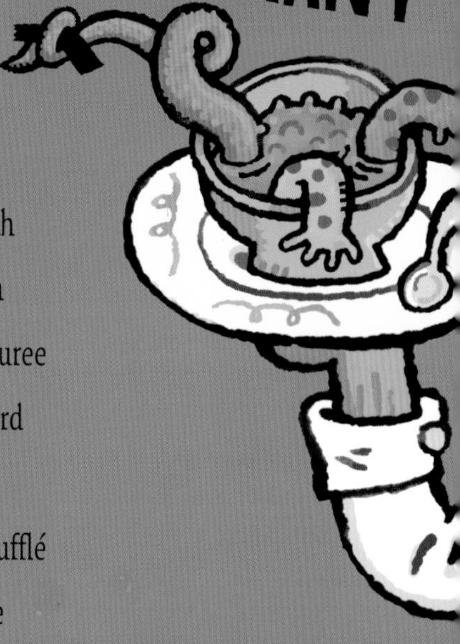

MENU

Beetle brain broth

Barbecued moth

Peppered piranha puree

Grasshopper gizzard

Liquefied lizard

Scorpion stinger soufflé

Wolverine waffle

Ferret falafel

Fricasseed skin of a snake

Skunk scat supreme

Head lice ice cream

Chocolate tarantula cake

PARASITE LOST

A hungry tapeworm deftly hooked

A pork chop (only partly cooked)

And rode into the cozy gut

Of nasty Norman Noodlebutt.

The worm would feast on Norman's dinner;

Norm, predictably, grew thinner,

Till, suspecting that he might

Be subject to a parasite,

He ate a stick of dynamite.

"That'll teach it," Norman gloated,

Smiled with pleasure—then exploded.

Moral:

Many lovely lives are ended

By consequences unintended.

NEVER BULLY A BUG

Young William was not nice to bugs,

Or bees, or centipedes, or slugs.

He'd poke, and pull, and squeeze, and tweak,

And laugh because they were so weak.

Young William never realized

The tiny mites he victimized

Had cousins that were giant-sized.

One day, while walking down the stair,

Young William met a bumblebear.

The bumblebear packed quite a sting,

But when a beast more frightening—

A stomping-mad rhinocepede—

Came hurtling toward him at top speed,

Young William, feeling far less smug,

Collided with a hipposlug,

And disappeared in one slow g - l - u - g.

LEAP HALLOWEEN

Every four hundred years there's a Leap Halloween,

When odd creatures appear that are not often seen,

Like the jelly-nosed nerbil, the long-eared brilloon,

The wobbly snoddler, the fancified gloon,

The burrowing bloatie, the quick-talking tick.

If you want to avoid them, I'll tell you the trick:

Just keep saying over and over and over,

"There is no such day as the 32nd of October."

MONSTER RESERVOIR

Someone left the gate ajar

At the monster reservoir,

Where dwell monsters yet unnamed,

Undocumented, and untamed,

Clamoring for your attention,

For beastly rhymes of *your* invention.

Take some paper, take a pen,

Take a breath, and now begin . . .